HIS NAME WAS SHORTLY FORTHCOMING

HOW CAPITAL LETTERS CAME TO BE

By Judy Steiner Grin

ISBN-13: 978-1546872900
ISBN-10: 1546872906
LCCN: 2017909375

For all my children, real and pretend.

ONCE THERE WAS A LAND WHERE THERE WERE NO capital letters.
not a name of a person or a book looked tall,
and one poor fox with a name worse than small
had the most perplexing problem of all.
his name was shortly forthcoming.

the fox had friends with names you would know.
ellie was an elephant from head to toe.
turtle, the turtle, looked like his name,

and prince was a tiger of jungle fame.

poor fox! his friends caused him trouble without meaning to,
but with his name not quite there yet, what could they do?
they said they'd call him shortly for short, or shortly for lunch,
but which one they meant was anyone's hunch,

and the fox, as confused as a fox could be,
was home all alone by the phone until three.

shortly forthcoming

prince looked for a mark or a sign made by the fox,
but there didn't seem to be one,
not even on his mail box.

they all went to school and things got even worse.
when the teacher asked for names, guess who she asked first?

"my name is shortly forthcoming!" he called from the back of the room.
the teacher said, "how long is shortly? forthcoming from whom?
you must have a name to write on your tag!"
and she made him a dunce cap from a paper bag.

now foxes are clever, they're supposed to be.
so he was determined to prove what his name should be.
the fox sat on the stool through a whole day of school
and thought and thought 'till he thought of a rule.

when he found a solution, he started to laugh.
he laughed so hard he doubled in half.
he then planned a party where he could show
the way first letters in names would change and grow.

ellie came first and soon prince came along.
they were both humming an alphabet song.
turtle came, as turtles do,
slowly, so slowly, and very late too.

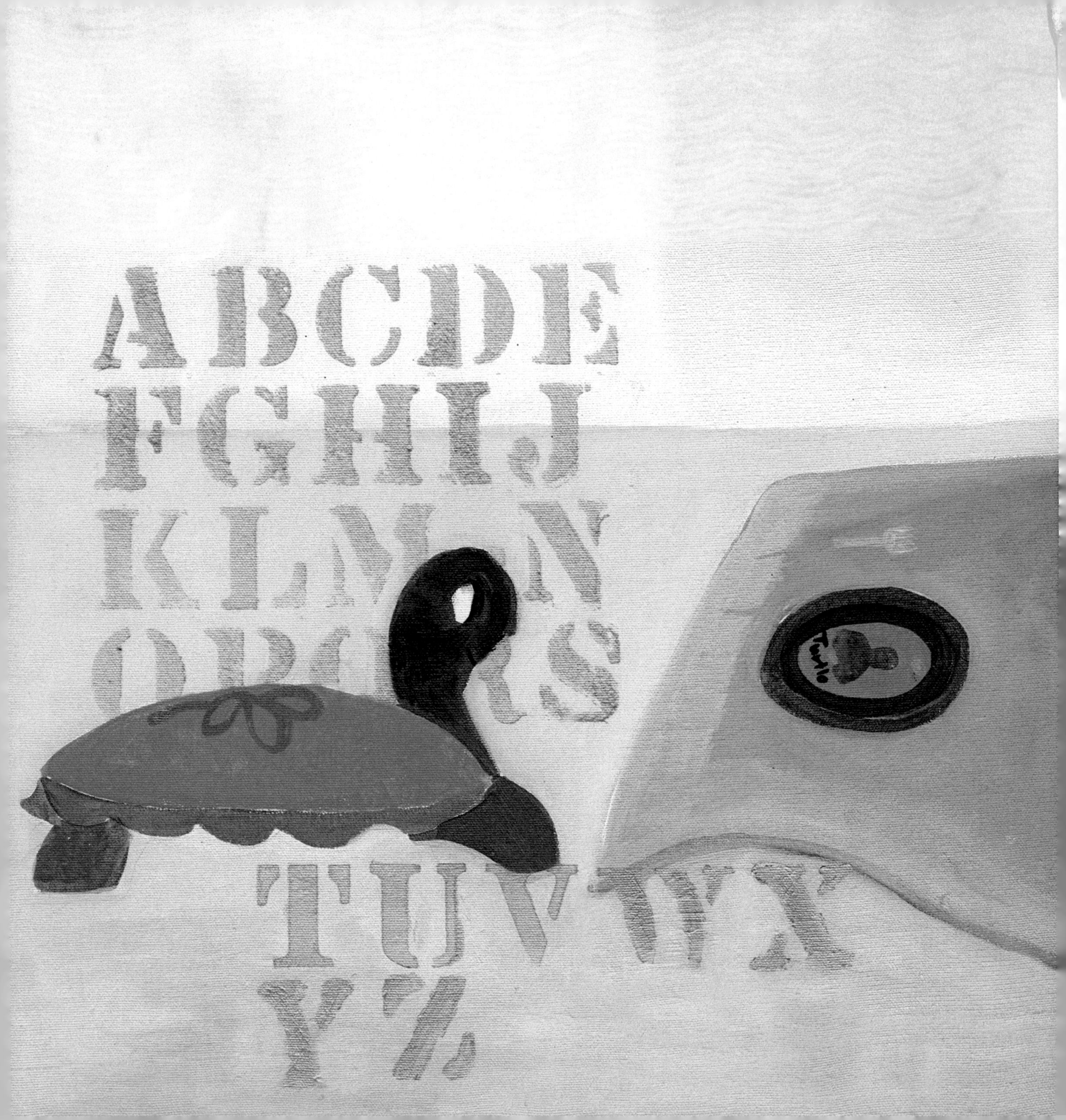
ABCDE
FGHIJ
TUVWX
YZ

inside, they saw their faces on plates.
under their faces were strange letters too,
their names were there, but they looked quite new.

"oooh, look," ellie said with glee. "could this really be me?"
"yup!" said the fox, "that's a capital e!"

turtle slowly found his place to be,
and prince said, "my first letter is bigger! yippee!"

"what does this mean and where is your place?"
they knew something was up by the smile on his face.

he then brought out a chart listing all sorts of names,
but they could see at a glance that each had been changed.

Name List

Before	After		Before	After
matthew	Matthew		ulrich	Ulrich
meredy	Meredy		uncle Wink	Uncle Wink
michael	Michael		valariano	Val
mildred	Mildred		violet	Violet
nancy	Nancy		wesley	Wesley
otto	Otto		yani	Yani
patricia	Pat		yvonne	Yvonne
prince	Prince		zelda	Zelda
quenton	Quenton			
rené	René			
roger	Roger			
ron	Ron			
ryan	Ryan			
sally	Sally			
shortly	Shortly			
sonny	Sonny			
susan	Susan			
tracie	Tracie			
turtle	Turtle			

New Letters

A B C D E F K I G H J L M N O P Q R T U W X S V Y Z

"look hard and look long, look one and look all, for the letters in names are no longer all small."

NEW RULES

Whenever a person or a place has a name, it's much more important and just not the same as ordinary words like coming or came.

Now make them better by changing the size and shape of the very first letter.

Use these new letters for people, titles, places, and for "i" when it's you. use them for roman numerals, initials, and to start new sentences too.

S.F.

amid shouts of good cheer, the fox raised his head and said,
"hoorah, hooray, i've just saved the day!
from now on my friends, by this special decree,
i'll be called Shortly Forthcoming, for that's really me!"

so many people liked the new law that it got out of hand.
they spread capital letters all over the land.
they used them as far as the eye could see
and that is how capitals came to be.

they used them for roman numerals and initials,
and finally the law was official.

It was then that the land with letters all small
didn't exist any more at all.

But how in the world did he get such a name?
Well, we still don't know, but it works just the same.

THE END

Made in the USA
Middletown, DE
16 November 2017